The Amazing Turkey Rescue

by Steve Metzger
Illustrated by Jim Paillot

SCHOLASTIC INC.
New York   Toronto   London   Auckland   Sydney
Mexico City   New Delhi   Hong Kong   Buenos Aires

It had been a great year for Ollie, Cassie, and Wing. They'd escaped from becoming Thanksgiving dinner on the farm, and were enjoying life on the loose.

The Amazing Turkey Rescue

To Nancy and Julia
—S.M.

For Molly, Jeff, Vinny, Riley, and Celery
—J.P.

ISBN-13: 978-0-545-01420-5
ISBN-10: 0-545-01420-4

12 11 10 9 8 7 6 5 4   8 9 10 11 12/0

Printed in the U.S.A.
First printing, October 2007

During the winter, they skied on Mount Baldy.

In the spring, they played baseball with the Turkey Legs.

When summer arrived, they hung three in Hawaii.

Now it was autumn again, just a few days before Thanksgiving. While the turkeys were busy jumping into a pile of leaves, a crow dropped a note on Cassie's hat. "Read this!" she squawked as she flew away.

"Oh, no!" Wing shouted. "It's the sheriff! He must have heard that we escaped and now he's coming to throw us in jail!"

"What does it say?" Ollie asked.

"It's not from the sheriff! It's from Pete the Chicken," Cassie said as she read the note.

Dear Ollie, Cassie, and Wing,

Help! There's a fox prowling around the chicken coop. You were smart enough to escape once, and now we really need you!

Your pal,
Pete the Chicken

"Wait a minute!" Wing yelled. "What if Farmer Joe catches us? Remember last Thanksgiving? I don't want to get eaten!"

"Wing makes a good point," Ollie said, nodding.

Cassie jumped up and down. "Don't you understand?" she said. "OUR FRIENDS ARE IN DANGER! We've got to do something!"

"You're right!" Wing said. "Let's go!"
They skipped.
They ran.
They gobbled.
Finally, they arrived at the wooden fence
surrounding the farm.

"Hey, there's Pete the Chicken!" Ollie called out. "Pssst, Pete."

Pete raced over. "You sure got here fast. Now put these on so Farmer Joe won't spot you," he said.

"We'll meet you behind the chicken coop in a few minutes," Cassie added.

When Pete left, Ollie jumped on top of Cassie, who jumped on top of Wing.

After a few clumsy attempts, they put on Farmer Joe's clothing. Wing wobbled over to the farm's entrance.

"Howdy," a friendly voice called out. "You must be one of the new workers."

Ollie said nothing.

"My name is Hank," the farmhand said. "What's yours?"

Again, silence. "Say something," whispered Cassie.

"Gobble," Ollie finally said.

"Gabby?" Hank said. "For someone named Gabby, you don't talk too much. What kind of work do you do?"

"Gobble," Ollie repeated.

"You cobble?" Hank said, scratching his head. "Oh, you're a cobbler! Well, we don't have many shoes that need fixing around here, but there must be some other kind of work you can do. I'll tell Farmer Kate you're here."

 As soon as Hank left, the three turkeys shed Farmer Joe's clothing and raced to the back of the chicken coop. There, waiting for them, was Pete the Chicken.

"The fox is about to pounce!" Pete warned.
"You've got to move fast!"

"I've got it!" yelled Cassie. "Here's the plan!" She whispered her idea to Ollie and Wing. "OK, let's go!"

Just as the fox was about to enter the chicken coop,
Ollie called out, "Wait! Don't take another step!"

The fox stopped and turned around. "Why not?"
he asked.

"Look at his color," Cassie said. "It's like a beautiful sunset."

"And those strong muscles," Wing added. "He'd be perfect!"

"Perfect for what?" the fox angrily asked. "Who are you anyway?"

"We're Mick, Mackie, and Moe, the famous Hollywood producers," Cassie replied.

"You might be perfect to star in our next movie," Wing added. "It's called *The Mighty Fox*."

"Do you really think I could be a movie star?" the fox asked. The turkeys huddled together.

"We're not sure," Cassie said.
"Let's see your teeth."
   The fox opened his jaws wide.

"They're, uh, pretty sharp," she said.

"Now let's check out his coordination," Ollie announced.
"How fast can you spin?"

The fox twirled around and around until he began to stagger.

"One more thing," Wing said. "Let's see how angry you can get."

Cassie and Ollie found a piece of rope and tied up the fox. He snarled, grunted, and howled. "Is that angry enough?" the fox asked.

"Yep, that's pretty angry," Cassie said. "And now you're going to be very angry."

"Why?" asked the fox.

"Because you're trapped!" Ollie shouted.

The fox screamed so loudly that everyone on the farm heard.

"Hey!" exclaimed Farmer Kate. "The turkeys who escaped last year are back!"

"And look!" said Farmer Joe. "They saved the chickens from a fox! They're heroes!"

"Hooray for the turkeys!" Farmer Kate and Farmer Joe cried. "You're welcome to live on the farm as long as you'd like."

As a special reward, the three turkeys were invited to join Farmer Joe and Farmer Kate's Thanksgiving feast, where they all ate…pizza!